The Big Story

Dominic Barker ■ **John Bradley**

The Norton Gazette

OXFORD
UNIVERSITY PRESS

Chapter 1

Day:	Monday
Time:	8:15 am
Location:	Jack Rico's bedroom

Meet Jack Rico. Age 10. Ace reporter. He looks in the mirror. Hair – too flat. Shirt – too neat. He spikes his hair and untucks his shirt. He grabs his notebook and his pen, opens his bedroom door and heads for the kitchen. "Today is the day I get to break a big story," he tells himself.

Jack's dream is to get a report he's written in *The Norton Gazette*. All he needs to do is find the right person and ask the right questions.

"You're going to be late for school," shouts his mum.

Jack runs down the stairs. He wouldn't be late for school if he had a new bike, but his mum won't let him have one.

"Can I have a new bike?" Jack asks.

His mum doesn't say anything. But she sighs. She's been asked that question before.

"I said, 'Can I have a new bike?'" repeats Jack.

His mum shakes her head.

"Why?"

"Because," says his mum.

"BOY NOT GIVEN GOOD ENOUGH ANSWER BY MOTHER," says Jack, who sometimes talks in headlines.

"It's the only answer you're getting," says his mum. "Sit down and eat your toast."

"Where's the jam?"

"We've run out. You'll have to make do with butter."

"BOY DENIED TOPPING OF CHOICE BY PARENT," observes Jack.

Chapter 2

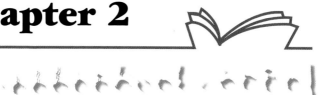

Day:	Monday
Time:	9:10am
Location:	Room 10, Norton School

Jack is sitting next to Molly, his best friend. She doesn't look too happy. "BEST FRIEND IN SAD FACE SHOCK," comments Jack. "What's up?"

Molly plonks a copy of *The Norton Gazette* on to the desk.

Deadly bug shuts pool

Terrified lifeguards rushed to shut down Norton Swimming Pool yesterday after health officer, Mr Arthur Pribit, discovered traces of a deadly bug. He commented, "I was doing routine tests on water samples when I spotted a strange result. There were signs of Cryptosporidiosis which can cause illness or even death." The pool was shut immediately and will stay closed until further notice.

The Gazette says: Well done, Arthur!

"Great story," says Jack.

"Glad you're seeing the good side," says Molly sarcastically.

"What's the matter?"

"The pool is where I train. There isn't another one for miles. It's the Under-11s County Championship in two weeks. If the pool stays shut, I've got no chance of winning."

"A follow-up story," says Jack, reaching for his notebook. "GIRL'S SWIMMING CAREER DESTROYED BY DEADLY BUG. I'll write it and take it to the *Gazette* after school. I knew this would be the day I'd finally get a story printed."

"I'm glad losing my chance in the championship makes you so happy."

"I'm not happy about it," says Jack. "But it's the news. I've got to report it. Just answer a few questions."

He picks up his pen.

"How does it feel to have your swimming career ruined before it's even begun?" Jack asks bluntly. Perhaps a little too bluntly.

Molly gives Jack a furious look.

"I'm not answering that," she snaps. "Report something that can get the pool re-opened if you want to be any help."

She stomps off to feed Gimli, the school hamster.

Chapter 3

Day:	Monday
Time:	4:35 pm
Location:	Offices of the Norton Gazette

"Another story, Jack?"

It's Veronica. Veronica is eighteen and a trainee reporter on the paper. She has to write all the stories nobody else wants to.

Jack nods. "It's a follow-up story about the pool. I'm waiting for Mr Richardson."

Veronica looks concerned. "He's in a bad mood today," she says. "Somebody spelt the mayor's name wrong on page two. She's been on the phone complaining all afternoon. Try another time maybe."

Jack doesn't want to go. This could be his big chance.

"I really think you should go," says Veronica.

But it's too late. The door of the Editor's office opens and a short round man with a moustache stalks out. Jeremy Richardson spots Jack straight away.

"What are you doing here again, Rico?" he demands. "This is a newspaper, not a playground."

"I've got a …"

"Don't tell me," says Richardson. "You've got another story."

Jack nods.

"And you expect me to waste my time reading it?"

"It might be quite good, Mr Richardson," suggests Veronica.

"Good?" snaps Richardson. "Don't you tell me what good is. I nearly had the front-page story on *The Daily World* once. That's no local paper. That's the biggest-selling paper in the whole country. *I'm* the one in this office who decides what good is."

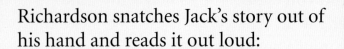

Richardson snatches Jack's story out of his hand and reads it out loud:

DEADLY BUG THREATENS SWIMMING CAREER

The news that Norton Pool is closed has ruined the training plans of Molly Green (aged 10) of Norton School. She was favourite to win the 50m freestyle but can no longer practise. Now she fears she will be defeated in the Under-11s County Championships. Molly was too upset to comment and was last seen crying on the school hamster.

"Do you want to print it?" Jack asks hopefully.

"Print it?" repeats Richardson. "This is the worst story I've ever read, Rico."

"Don't say that, Mr Richardson," protests Veronica.

"Don't tell *me* what to say and what not to say. There's nothing in this story. She might win, she might lose. You haven't even got a quote from her. There's no drama here, Rico."

"She wouldn't answer my questions," explains Jack, "so I put in the bit about crying on the hamster to make the reader sympathise with her."

"Crying on a hamster?" shouts Richardson. "That's not news. Eating a hamster is news. Crying on one is just weird." He scrunches the story into an ugly ball and throws it expertly into the bin. "I don't want to see you back here," he says pointing a stubby finger at Jack. "Some people can write stories and some people can't. And you, Rico, are one of the people who can't." Richardson stomps back into his office and slams the door.

Jack can't believe it. He thought the story had everything – hope, sport … hamsters.

"BOY'S DREAMS BROKEN BY CRUEL EDITOR," says Jack.

"Perhaps this will make you feel better," says Veronica, taking something out of her pocket.

"What is it?"

"A mini tape recorder. You can use it to tape interviews."

"Are you sure?"

"Yeah. I've got two."

"BOY JUMPS FOR JOY AT SURPRISE GIFT!" says Jack. "Thanks."

"Better luck next time!"

Day:	Tuesday
Time:	9:10 am
Location:	Assembly hall, Norton School

"Settle down, children," says Miss Targett. "Today is a special day." Miss Targett is wearing her best red suit.

Molly sits down next to Jack. "HAS EX-SWIMMER FORGIVEN BEST FRIEND?" Jack asks.

Molly doesn't say anything.

"I'll take that as 'no comment'," Jack says.

"Jack Rico! Are you talking?" shouts Miss Targett. Everybody turns to look at Jack.

"Are we on the record?" he asks Miss Targett.

"I beg your pardon, Rico?"

"On the record, I wasn't talking," explains Jack. "Off the record, I was."

Miss Targett gives Jack one of her Stares.

"You're very lucky, Jack Rico. We've got a special guest here so I'm not going to tell you off. But I've got my eye on you."

Jack decides to be good. At least until she takes that eye off him.

"Today," says Miss Targett, "we're very fortunate to have a visitor. Please welcome Mr Howard, owner of UltraGym."

Mr Howard walks to the front of the assembly hall. He's wearing a blue shirt but no tie and the biggest smile Jack has ever seen. The only time he's seen more teeth was in a shark's mouth.

"Hi, kids!"

"Hello, Mr Howard," they chorus back.

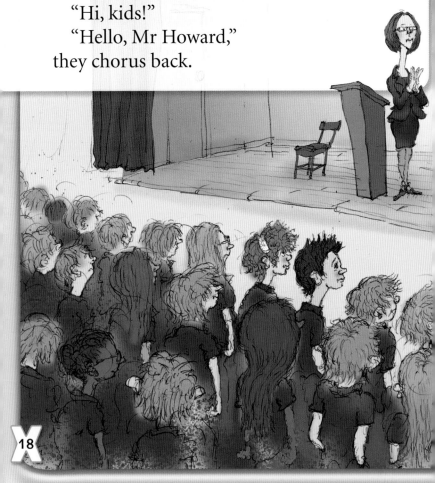

"No, no," says Mr Howard. "Don't call me Mr Howard. Call me Dave. I want you, your parents and your teachers to think of me as a friend. I'm everybody's friend."

"MAN WITH BIG TEETH WANTS TO BE YOUR FRIEND," whispers Jack to Molly.

Molly smiles and then remembers she's angry with Jack and stops.

"Today I want to talk to you about health, exercise and UltraGym," says Dave. "UltraGym has just opened and it's a state-of-the-art fitness centre. It's very important that you and your parents get lots of exercise and at UltraGym we aim to provide that. Now that the town swimming pool is closed…"

Molly sighs regretfully.

"…UltraGym has the only swimming pool for miles around. So tell your parents they should join immediately. UltraGym is great value for money. Thank you."

Miss Targett stands up. "Aren't you forgetting something, Mr Howard?"

"Am I?"

Miss Targett gives Mr Howard one of her stares.

"Oh, yes," he says. "We at UltraGym believe in children doing exercise and being healthy and growing up to be adults who join UltraGym. Therefore we are donating a hundred pounds worth of high-quality sports equipment to the school. Remember, at UltraGym we care. Thank you." Dave Howard and his big smile sit down.

"I'm sure we'd all like to say thank you to Mr Howard for his generous donation, wouldn't we, children?" says Miss Targett.

The children know what they have to do.

"Thank you, Mr Howard," they all chorus obediently.

"Now," says Miss Targett, "please wait quietly. Mr Richardson from the local paper is here to take a picture."

Mr Richardson walks forward, clutching a camera in one hand and a notebook and pencil in the other.

He seems very different from the man who was so horrible to Jack yesterday. "Hello, children," he says cheerfully. "Mr Howard has put a large ad in the paper this week for UltraGym so we want to make sure there's a good story and picture to go with it. Mr Howard, could you stand in front of the children? Everybody smile – one … two … three …" FLASH!

Moments later Dave Howard and Mr Richardson were getting into their cars and driving away.

Chapter 5

Day: Wednesday
Time: 10:15 am
Location: Locker room,
Norton School

Norton's kids say "yes" to UltraGym

Yesterday was great at Norton School. Children cheered when Dave Howard, local businessman, announced he would be donating sports equipment worth thousands of pounds to the school. One child, Jack Rico, said, "Mr Howard is my hero. Everyone should join UltraGym." His friend Molly added, "I'm glad the local swimming pool is shut. Now I can make my parents take me to UltraGym." Friendly Dave stayed behind after assembly, signing autographs for the children. "I don't mind," says Dave. "I'll do anything to keep kids healthy".

The GAZETTE says: Dave's a local hero.

"That didn't happen," says Jack, reading the article in disbelief. "I never said that."

"Talking to yourself, Rico?"

Jack looks up. All the other boys are already changed and gone. Standing over him is Mr Morris, the PE teacher.

"I was just …"

"Reading," says Mr Morris. "This is PE. Time to stop reading and start running. You can carry out this bag. It's got the new equipment from UltraGym."

Jack picks up the bag. It's heavy.

"BOY SUES SCHOOL AFTER INJURING BACK," he mutters.

Outside, Jack's class is lined up on the playground. "Today we get to use the new equipment sent by UltraGym," Mr Morris tells them. He reaches into the bag and pulls out a basketball. "Wonderful!" he says. "We need a new basketball." He bounces it on the ground. It doesn't bounce back.

"It's got a puncture," says Molly.

Mr Morris looks at the flat basketball with disappointment. "Probably got put in by accident," he says. "What else is in here?"

He tries again. "I can feel a tennis racket," he says. "We could really do with … oh!" Mr Morris pulls out a tennis racket. Half the strings are missing. He yanks out a discus. It's warped. "This is all rubbish." Mr Morris dumps the bag on the ground.

"Excuse me, Mr Morris."

"What is it, Rico?"

"Miss Targett says you shouldn't drop rubbish in the playground."

Chapter 6

Day: Wednesday
Time: 4:45pm
Location: Offices of The Norton Gazette

"Veronica, I told you not to let him in here again!"

"He said it was important, Mr Richardson."

"I wanted to ask you about the story in today's *Gazette*," says Jack quickly.

"I wrote that," Richardson tells him. "Brilliant, wasn't it?"

"Er …" Jack hesitates. "It wasn't true."

"Of course it was true," replies Richardson.

"The amount of money was wrong, nobody wanted Mr Howard's autograph, and Molly and I didn't say those things you wrote."

"You said 'thank you'," says Richardson. "That's the same thing. Do you think I've got time to run around interviewing children? I'm a busy man. Go and play with your new PE equipment."

"That's what I wanted to tell you," says Jack. "It's all rubbish. The basketball is flat and the tennis racket is …"

"Are you trying to make me look stupid, Rico?"

"No. I just thought …"

"This morning," says Richardson, "I wrote that Dave Howard is a local hero. I'm not going to write the complete opposite tomorrow because of one popped basketball."

Without waiting for an answer, Richardson stomps back to his office.

"RICO SORRY IF VERONICA'S IN TROUBLE WITH BAD-TEMPERED BOSS," Jack says.

"I don't care," says Veronica. "He's always shouting. Any new job offer and I'm out of here."

"Good luck!"

"Thanks," says Veronica. "What about you? Where are you going next with your story?"

"Don't know," says Jack. "REPORTER HITS DEAD END."

"You can't think like that," Veronica tells him. "A reporter never gives up. Keep digging and see what you find."

"Where should I dig?"

"If it was me," says Veronica, "I'd take a trip to UltraGym."

Chapter 7

Day: Wednesday
Time: 5:30 pm
Location: UltraGym

"Welcome to UltraGym. My name is Sally. Would you like to join? You can swim, work out or simply chill at our juice bar."

Standing behind the reception desk, Sally wears a blue UltraGym uniform. She gives Jack exactly the same smile she gave to the previous ten people. Jack noticed that they all became members. Lots of them mentioned the article and said what a good man Dave Howard must be. Jack wonders what they'd think if they saw the broken PE equipment.

"Could I see Mr Howard?" asks Jack.

"Mr Howard is busy."

"I have a few things I want to ask him about the sports equipment he …"

The phone rings. "Excuse me a moment," says Sally.

Jack knows that you shouldn't listen in to other people's phone calls. But he isn't really listening. He's just standing nearby with his ears open.

"Hello, UltraGym." The caller says something. "I'm afraid Mr Howard is too busy to talk right now." The caller says something else. Loudly.

Sally winces. "Please don't shout at me, Mr Pribit. I didn't realise it was you. I'll connect you immediately." Sally puts the phone call through. Then she looks at Jack. "Swim, work out or chill?"

Jack doesn't answer. He's just remembered where he heard the name Pribit before – in the article about the swimming pool closing. Why is Mr Pribit phoning Mr Howard? And why does he get put through when nobody else does? "STRANGE GOINGS ON AT ULTRAGYM," thinks Jack.

Suddenly, out of his office comes
Mr Howard. Yesterday's big shark smile
has vanished.

"Key to the safe please, Sally," he snaps.

"Mr Howard," says Jack.

"I'm very busy."

"But I just have a few …"

"I *said,* I'm very busy." Mr Howard doesn't
even bother looking at Jack. Now that there
are no reporters around to take photos, he
doesn't need to be nice to a kid.

He grabs the key from Sally, picks up a backpack and goes over to the safe. Jack can see the big pile of banknotes inside. Mr Howard grabs a large handful and stuffs them into the backpack. "I'll be about an hour, Sally." Mr Howard pushes his way through the revolving doors and out into the street.

Sally watches him go. Then she remembers she has a customer. "Swim, work out or chill?"

But there's nobody to answer her question. Jack has gone.

Chapter 8

Day: Wednesday
Time: 5:40 pm
Location: Norton Park

Dave Howard charges down the main street, tightly clutching his backpack to his chest. He turns left at some traffic lights and then right soon after. He walks faster and faster, holding the backpack tighter and tighter. He's looking at everybody. After all, he's carrying a lot of money and someone might be a thief.

It makes it hard for Jack to follow him. He has to duck behind a wall, then hide behind a tree, then pretend to be bending over tying his laces.

When he looks up, there's no sign of Howard. Jack can't believe he's lost him. This could be his last chance to find out what's happening. He dashes down the street, his head darting frantically from side to side. Just in time, he spots Howard slipping into Norton Park. Jack's not going to lose him again. He sprints into the park.

Norton Park

PARK

Howard's walking towards the lake. The ducks start quacking, hoping for bread, but Howard ignores them. He goes straight to a bench, sits down and places the backpack next to him. There's another man already sitting there. He doesn't even look at Howard. Anybody passing by would think they were strangers just sharing a bench. But Jack isn't anyone. He remembers who the person is from the picture in Monday's paper: Arthur Pribit.

Jack hides behind a tree to see what happens. Nothing.

For five long minutes, Dave Howard and Arthur Pribit look at the ducks. Jack can't believe it. Are they both just birdwatchers?

Then, suddenly, without even glancing at Howard, Pribit leans over, picks up the backpack, looks inside, nods and puts it down next to himself. Howard, who'd been holding onto the backpack so tightly all the way to the park, doesn't even seem to notice. Weird.

Now, Jack can see that they're talking to each other. But not like people normally talk. They don't look at each other. Jack would give anything to be able to hear what they're saying. Maybe it's the key to breaking the story.

Then he remembers the mini-tape recorder! If he could just slip it under the bench, perhaps he could record what they're saying. But there's a problem. How can he get the tape recorder close enough without Howard and Pribit noticing? Jack needs an excuse to go scrambling behind the bench. And he hasn't got one. "BUDDING REPORTER WATCHES HELPLESSLY AS STORY SLIPS AWAY," sighs Jack.

Chapter 9

Day:	Wednesday
Time:	5:55 pm
Location:	Norton Park

Suddenly, there's a shout behind Jack. Two boys are playing football. Jack has an idea.

He switches the tape recorder on and hides it in his hand. Then he pops out from behind the tree and jogs over to them. "Can I play?"

"OK," says one boy, kicking the ball over to him. "Pass it here."

Jack boots the ball as hard as he can towards the bench where Howard and Pribit are sitting.

The boy looks at him in disbelief. "That's the worst pass I've ever seen," he says.

"Sorry," says Jack. "I'll go and get it." Jack charges after the ball. He has to catch it before it goes past the two men. Jack runs faster than he's ever run before. He reaches the ball just as it rolls under the bench.

"What are you doing?" shouts Howard angrily.

"Sorry," says Jack, bending down to pick up the ball. He leaves the tape recorder in its place.

Jack passes the ball to the other boys with surprising skill for someone whose last pass was the worst anyone had ever seen. "You're right," he tells them. "Maybe football's not my game." And he slips back behind the tree.

Howard and Pribit are still talking. But Jack's got new worries. The ducks decide to investigate the bench. Jack watches as they quack around the two men's feet. What if they ruin the tape? What if they eat his tape recorder? "DUCKS FOIL RICO'S PLAN," Jack groans to himself.

Then, without warning, Pribit and Howard stand up and walk off in different directions. Pribit takes the backpack. As soon as they're out of sight, Jack runs to the bench to get the tape recorder. The ducks haven't damaged it but has it picked up the conversation?

Chapter 10

Day: Wednesday
Time: 8:00 pm
Location: Offices of The Norton Gazette

Two hours later. Jack arrives at *The Norton Gazette* offices, clutching a story in his hand. Veronica is just about to lock up for the night.

"Is Mr Richardson still here?" asks Jack.

"He's gone home."

"But I've got a really big story!"

"And I've got a date with a good-looking photographer," says Veronica. "Bring it back tomorrow."

"But it's really, really big."

Veronica sighs. "OK," she says. "Let me read it."

Veronica opens the door and goes back into the office, her eyes getting bigger and bigger with every word she reads.

"You see," says Jack.

"Ssssh," Veronica hushes him. "Let me finish it."

Jack can't bear the waiting. Every second that passes feels like a minute. Finally, Veronica puts down the story.

"So," says Jack, "have I done it? Do you think this story will get in the *Gazette*?"

Veronica shakes her head.

"But …"

"Let me make a phone call or two," Veronica tells him. "I might be able to sort out something."

"What about the good-looking photographer?"

"Now I come to think about it," grins Veronica, "he isn't that good-looking!"

Chapter 11

Day:	Thursday
Time:	8:10 am
Location:	Jack Rico's house

There's a clunk as *The Daily World* plops onto the mat. Jack's mum picks it up and carries it into the kitchen. She's surprised to see Jack already sitting there eating his toast.

"Can I have a new bike?" asks Jack.

"It was 'no' on Monday. It's still 'no'. There's nothing you could say to convince me."

"How about if I say I'll buy it myself?"

His mum looks suspicious. "How would you get the money for a new bike?"

"SCHOOL BOY BREAKS MAJOR STORY IN NATIONAL NEWSPAPER," Jack answers.

His mum bursts out laughing. "Nice try, Jack," she tells him. "*The Daily World* is the biggest selling paper in the country. They don't take …" She glances at the front page and stops. "What's your name doing on this story?"

It's Jack's turn to laugh. He's laughing so hard he almost can't hear her reading the story out loud.

The Daily World

Swimming pool fraud

by Jack Rico

The Daily World has uncovered a disgraceful fraud in Norton. Dishonest businessman, Mr David Howard, bribed health inspector, Mr Arthur Pribit, to fake results of a water-quality test to ensure the local swimming pool was closed down.

Mr Howard hoped to force people to join his expensive gym because there would be nowhere else in the area to swim. Howard and Pribit refused to comment. The police expect to make arrests later today.

The Daily World says: The sooner, the better.

Jack's mum puts down the paper. She's got a big smile on her face. "I guess we'll be going to the bike shop after school."

There's a knock on the front door. The phone rings at the same time.

"You do the door," says Jack's mum. "I'll do the phone."

Standing on the doorstep is Molly. "Want to walk to school?"

"I thought you were mad at me."

"Not since they re-opened the pool because of what you wrote," Molly tells him. "I've still got enough time to train to win the race."

"Jack," says his mum, appearing with the phone in her hand. "It's for you."

"Hello?" says Jack.

"Rico," says a familiar voice. "This is Mr Richardson from the *Gazette*. We've always been buddies, haven't we? I know I make jokes about your stories but I've always thought very highly of your ability."

"You never told me," says Jack.

"No," admits Richardson, "but I always thought it. And this story in *The Daily World* just shows how right I was. Anyway we're a bit short-staffed at the moment. Veronica's been offered a job on *The Daily World* out of the blue and she's taken it. So there's nobody to cover the swimming championship next week. I was wondering if you could do it for me."

"Hmmm," says Jack, "I'm quite busy."

"Please," begs Richardson. "I really need you."

EDITOR

"I suppose I can do it," Jack tells him. "After all, I've always wanted a story in the *Gazette*."

Jack hangs up the phone. "You sure you're going to win that race, Molly?"

Molly nods.

"So how do you want to be described in the *Gazette*?"

"What?"

Jack grins mischievously. "I was thinking 'lucky'."

"Lucky?" says Molly. "More like 'brilliant'!"

"Painfully slow?"

"Seriously fast!"

"Awkward?"

"Graceful!"

Still disagreeing, the two best friends set off for school.